Solomon's Secret

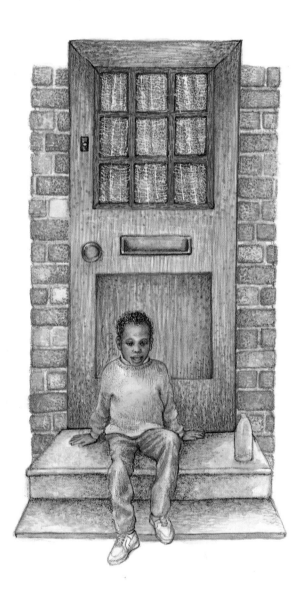

Solomon's Secret

Saviour Pirotta
pictures by Helen Cooper

Dial Books for Young Readers · New York

Solomon lived down the street from
Mr. and Mrs. Zee.

   Hardly anyone saw the Zees on weekends.
Their garden grew wild, spreading into the street.
And sometimes strange music, the sound of unusual
instruments, floated out from their backyard.
It seemed as if the Zees lived in a country
all their own.

Sometimes neighborhood kids threw rocks at the Zees' front door.

"Maybe they're crazy," Lorna said.

"Maybe they're Martians," Stan called. "Maybe they'll eat us if we get too close."

But Solomon didn't join in. He knew the real answer. Solomon knew the secret.

It had all started the summer before, when Solomon and his dad baked cinnamon rolls. "Why don't we give some to the Zees?" his dad said. "I'm sure they'd like them. You could take them over there, Solomon."

Then he put some rolls on a plate and covered them with a napkin.

Solomon didn't really want to go, but his dad said, "They're good people, Solomon."

The house was quiet when Solomon rang
the bell. Mrs. Zee opened the door.
"Hello, Solomon," she said. "Come on in."

Inside the house was cozy and warm.

"Good to see you, Solomon," said Mr. Zee. "You're just in time for dessert. How about some fresh pie to go with those cinnamon rolls?"

"And pastries from India—they'd be delicious with tea," Mrs. Zee said.

Solomon noticed a copper kettle on the stove, shining brighter than any he'd ever seen. "It looks too special for just boiling water," he said.

"It *is* special, Solomon," Mr. Zee told him. "It has magic to send us far and wide, as long as we're back before the water boils!"

Mrs. Zee picked up the gleaming kettle. "It will take a while yet. Why don't you two fetch the rest of the treats?"

Solomon followed Mr. Zee through a creaky door into the backyard. He had never seen such tall stalks of rhubarb before. "What are we looking for?" Solomon asked.

"A trail of paw prints," said Mr. Zee. "Not dog prints, of course. Those would just take us around the garden. What we need is something that will take us farther—something like a trail of panda prints."

Solomon found a panda print beneath the branches of a willow tree.

"The trail starts here," said Mr. Zee. "We'd better hurry. We mustn't keep Lin Ho waiting."

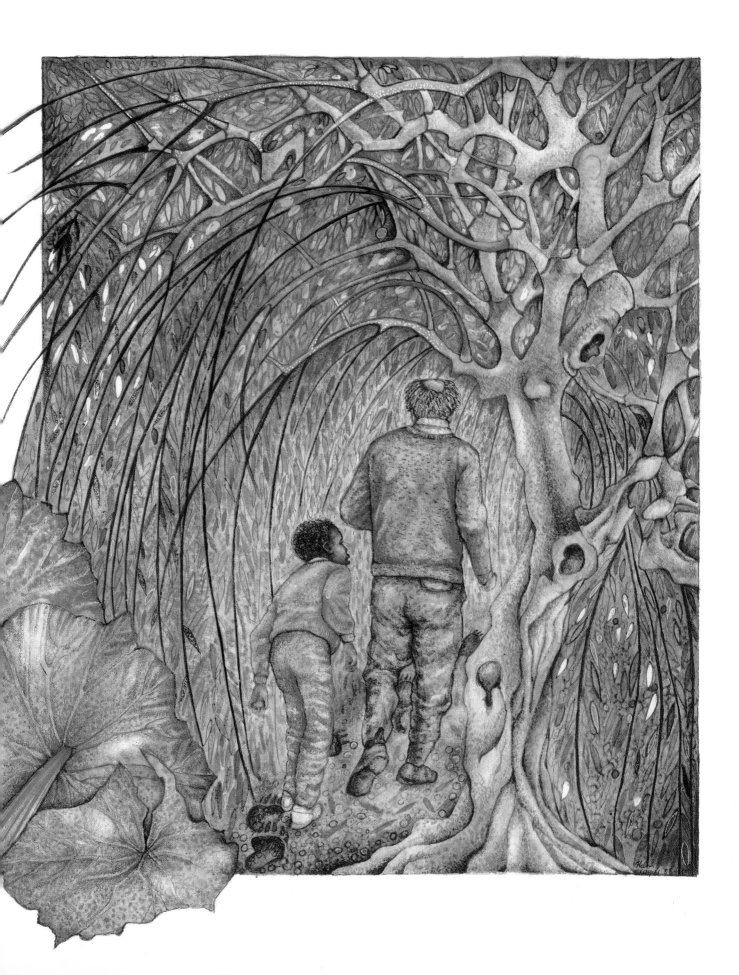

Solomon trotted after Mr. Zee.

The panda trail stretched all the way through the rhubarb stalks, past a huge mountain, and over a bridge covered by willows.

At the other end of the trail was a small village with children playing in the streets.

"Welcome to China," said Lin Ho. "Here is your tea."

"Thank you," said Mr. Zee. He paid Lin Ho and led Solomon back along the trail to the rhubarb garden.

"Now we need a trail of tiger prints," he said.

Solomon saw a strange mark in the mud between the little duck pond and the holly bush.

"Could this be it?" he asked Mr. Zee. Mr. Zee nodded.

The tiger trail took them across a deep valley, past a large palace with ivory towers.

They followed it down a narrow street with delicious
smells wafting out from the windows. "Tiger trails,"
said Mr. Zee, "always lead to special places."

The woman in the shop was wearing a bright sari.

"Hello, Mrs. Rai," said Mr. Zee. "This is Solomon."

"Welcome to India," she said, smiling. "What will it be today? Some fresh *jalebis*?"

Solomon saw the pastries glistening with syrup. "Yes, please. They smell delicious."

Mr. Zee counted out ten rupees and thanked Mrs. Rai. He let Solomon carry the hot jalebis back to the garden.

Soon the two of them were looking for
the tracks of a roadrunner. "Here they are!"
cried Solomon.
The roadrunner trail took them past some
tall cactus under the hot sun.

It led right to a small bakery in the middle of the desert. "Best pumpkin pie in the whole United States," said Mr. Cole.

"Thank you," said Mr. Zee. He and Solomon hurried back to the rhubarb garden.

"You're just in time for a nice cup of hot tea," said Mrs. Zee. "Are you hungry?"

"I'm starving," Solomon said.

Mr. Zee and Solomon put the pumpkin pie and the jalebis on the table.

Mr. Zee cut the pie and Mrs. Zee gave each of them a plate. "You're welcome to come again next Saturday," she told Solomon as he took a big bite. "It'll be our secret."

Mr. Zee poured Solomon some tea.

"Next time, we may find a boa constrictor's trail," he said. "Who knows where that might lead?"

To Martin Cowell and Vicki
H.C.

First published in the United States
by Dial Books for Young Readers
A Division of Penguin Books USA Inc.
2 Park Avenue
New York, New York 10016

Published in Great Britain
by Methuen Children's Books,
a division of OPG Services, Ltd.
Text copyright © 1989 by Saviour Pirotta
Pictures copyright © 1989 by Helen Cooper
Printed in Belgium
First Edition
N
2 4 6 8 10 9 7 5 3 1
Library of Congress Cataloging in Publication Data
Pirotta, Saviour.
Solomon's secret / by Saviour Pirotta:
illustrated by Helen Cooper.
p. cm.
Summary: When Solomon visits his neighbors Mr. and Mrs. Zee
for afternoon tea, he discovers their backyard harbors
exotic adventure and limitless possibilities.
ISBN 0-8037-0694-4
[1. Neighborliness—Fiction. 2. Blacks—Fiction.]
I. Cooper, Helen (Helen F.), ill. II. Title.
PZ7.P6425So 1989 [Fic]—dc19 88-38461 CIP AC